The
FOOTBALL'S
REVOLT

pictures and words
by

LEWITT-HIM

V&A Publishing

There are many famous football teams in the world, but the most famous and most clever is the team of Goalbridge. At least, this is what the people of Goalbridge say. On the other hand, the people of Kickford maintain that this cannot be true, because there is not a better team than Kickford.

Last year Kickford was beaten by Goalbridge, but it was only due to the fact that the famous Kickford captain, named O'Kay, who plays back, was not at his best. Shortly before the match started he had eaten too much steak. But to-day, being the day of the annual match for the Silver Cup, O'Kay's team, say the people of Kickford, will show what they really can do.

Kickford has 3,553 residents and Goalbridge 3,556. But on this day both towns were completely deserted, because all the inhabitants had left for the football ground. First to leave were the two teams. They drove slowly, in wagons drawn by very fat horses, and they felt very proud of themselves in their Extra-Special Jerseys, which were only worn for the Silver Cup Match. For the rest of the year they were preserved in glass cases in the Town Halls, and people paid sixpence to come and look at them. The teams were followed by the Referee, on his scooter; by the Mayors, in their big cars, and by all the Kickforders and Goalbridgers with their wives and children, with rugs, cushions, prams and sandwiches. This was the match they had been expecting for so long. There was nobody left in the towns but the firemen, who had to see that the dogs did not fight the cats, and the cats did not eat the canaries.

There it was, the lovely green playing-ground with the goal-posts and the white lines. Around the ground were stands for the spectators. In one special box one could see the Mayors, and in the grand-stand the Townsmen who had been careful to buy their tickets in good time. Outside the ground were trees, on which sat the thoughtless ones who came too late to get tickets. The seats in the trees have always, in the past, been reserved for the little boys of Goalbridge and Kickford, but to-day these places were filled by strong and determined men, so that the poor little boys had to remain at the foot of the trees and could not see a thing. After a bit, the boys decided to go off to the common near by, and to play their own match with an old ball that O'Kay had given to his son William.

As soon as they left, the band started playing and the two famous teams marched on to the ground. The proud Kickfords in blue shirts, and the champion Goalbridges in yellow and brown.

The captains of the two teams politely shook hands. The onlookers settled down more comfortably on their cushions and in the branches of the trees, and unpacked their sandwiches. Mr. Rembrandt took a fine photograph of the whole group. The followers of Kickford sang their war-cry: "Hey-Dey, we win, O'Kay!"; the followers of Goalbridge shouted: "Huck-Puck, a Goal for Goalbridge!" The Referee blew a loud blast on his whistle. The Mayor of Kickford kicked off, and the match started.

The forwards attacked furiously, the backs defended like Trojans, and the goalkeepers jumped like monkeys; the ball jumped from head to head, and rebounded from foot to foot. Goalbridge shouted, "Goal," and Kickford cried out, "Foul." The Referee blew his whistle. The spectators ate their sandwiches, chocolates, and biscuits. And everybody was very, very contented.

The only unhappy one was the poor football, which was being kicked harder than he ever remembered. But nobody bothered about him, because, after all, he was nothing but a football, who could not even talk English. And so they pushed, beat, and kicked him from one corner of the field to the other, from one goal to the other, from forward to forward, half-back to back, back to goalkeeper. Twenty-two strong men against one little ball.

This is the ladder used
by the strong and
determined men
to climb the trees

The ball became more and more furious, because the men kicked him harder and harder. He was most furious with O'Kay, because it was he who kicked him the hardest. At last the ball said, "Oufff," which meant in ball language, "Go easy." But nobody took any notice of it, because nobody understood the language of footballs. Besides, everybody was very excited, because O'Kay had got hold of the ball once more and was about to send it into the opponents' goal with one of his usual magnificent kicks.

The crowd was sitting there hardly breathing at all. It even forgot to eat its sandwiches.

Well, on this day the football had endured a great deal, but now the terrible kick he got surpassed anything he had felt before. Screaming with pain, he flew higher and higher and . . . *did not come down again.* There he was, hanging in the sky, murmuring: "Pumppff, fumffpp," which means in the football language: "Now go on without me, gentlemen, I won't have this treatment any longer. I just stay here, where it is rather windy, but where, at least, there are no brutal O'Kays." And with perfect peace of mind he sat down on a passing cloud.

The 3,556 residents of Goalbridge and the 3,553 of Kickford, with the exception of the firemen who had been staying at home, stared with open mouths towards the sky, and waited impatiently for the ball to return. But the ball stayed where it was.

"What do you think of that?" said the Referee, and looked helplessly at both captains. And they looked helplessly at him, and said: "One ought to do something about it, don't you think?" And the Referee replied: "Wait until I put on my

glasses, because, without them, I can't read the Rules." So he put on his glasses and read hard, while everybody waited anxiously. "I have got it," he said at last. "We must have another ball." "Of course," shouted the captains. "But we have not got another ball, and also, we can't buy one because it is Thursday and all shops are closed."

"That is right," whispered the confused Referee. "I completely forgot that. I must think about it again."

He put on his glasses again, and pondered deeply. And the players sat around him in a circle and pondered just as deeply. So much so that the sweat ran down their foreheads and dropped on to the grass.

The two Mayors in their box, the football fans in their stands, and the strong and determined men in the trees . . . all were sitting and thinking very hard.

All except O'Kay, who stole away to his son William. William was playing with his old football with the other boys on the common. O'Kay knew because he had given him the

old football for his tenth birthday present.

"William," he called, "I am sorry to disturb you, but you must help us. We have lost our football, and now all the players are sitting there and thinking where they are going to get another ball. And if they keep on thinking much longer, they will become so ill that they will never be able to get on with their match."

"Well," said young William O'Kay, "if you take our football, how can we finish our own game?"

O'Kay thought very hard.

"I tell you what, you can come and watch ours."

"O.K., dad," said William. And O'Kay returned to the ground with all the boys and the old football. But there were no seats empty except in the Mayors' box. So the Mayors had to make room for the boys, who thus had the best seats.

"Here comes the ball," sang the boys. "Here comes the ball," shouted the onlookers. "Where is the ball?" asked the yawning footballers, because so much thinking had made them very sleepy. "Here comes the ball," cried the Referee. He took off his glasses, played a note on his whistle, and kicked the ball into the field.

The Mayors' cigars

Once more the match began and the footballers kicked the new ball eagerly. They bumped it, threw it, and kicked it all over the field. The public shouted, the Referee blew his whistle, the Mayors smoked their cigars contentedly, and the boys in the Mayors' box swung their legs with joy. The strong and determined men in the trees stretched their necks to be able to watch things better, and all were very happy. All had entirely forgotten the first football, which still sat on his cloud above the field.

But when Mr. O'Kay got William's football, and once again kicked with his usual force high into the sky, it came very near to the first football, which cried out in the football language: "I say, do come here." Then the two footballs greeted one another and began to talk about the bad players. They talked a great deal about hard boots and still harder heads, but mostly they talked about the wicked O'Kay, their arch enemy No. 1. And they hovered up and down above the ground whilst talking, with not the least intention of returning to the field.

All the people below stared angrily towards the balls and shouted: "There is something wrong." The footballers were furious and reproached one another, and the Referee looked in his pockets for his glasses, because he thought: "I will have to look at the Rules again."

But young O'Kay leant out of the Mayors' box and shouted as loud as he could: "Why don't you make a pyramid like acrobats and get the balls?" "Little boys should be seen and not heard, and must not disturb their elders when thinking," replied the Referee, who was very indignant. "I have a wonderful idea of my own," he said, "what do you think of making a pyramid like acrobats?"

"Wonderful indeed," said the footballers, and ran to the pavilion to fetch tables, benches, and chairs, to make the pyramid. And O'Kay took even the little box in which Mrs. Plump always sat and sold the tickets.

They put the little box in the middle of the field, piled tables, benches, and chairs on top of it and then a few of the strongest men climbed to the top. Others stood on their shoulders and others again climbed on to their shoulders, and

O'Kay climbed higher than all the others and held a cane chair in his hand. Then the Referee crept up to the cane chair. Gasping, he stood on his toes and tried to catch the footballs, which were very, very near him.

However, the balls laughed to themselves and went up higher still. This made the Referee absolutely mad, and he asked for a broom to get the balls. But when he had nearly reached them, a fly suddenly settled on his nose and, in brushing it away, he slid, and then the whole wonderful pyramid lost its balance and crashed with terrific noise and shouts to the ground. Referee, broom, chairs, captains, tables, benches, forwards, half-backs, backs, ticket box, and goal-keepers, everybody and everything was lying about on the ground in absolute confusion, while the two footballs looked smilingly down on them from the sky.

17

This is the fly
responsible for
the crash

"Foul," said the players, making sure they were unhurt. "Foul," said O'Kay, whose legs only could be seen, because in falling he crashed through the roof of the ticket box. "Foul," said the Referee, angrily, as he threw off the cane chair, which was hanging round his neck like a frill. "I was just saying this was going to happen to the pyramid. And now my glasses are broken, and I can't think any more."

But young O'Kay shouted: "Don't think so much. Call for the fire brigade." And the Referee was very offended, and said: "The youth of to-day have not the slightest respect for great thinkers like me. Again and again they make their silly suggestions." And immediately he called for the fire brigade.

The firemen, of course, were very pleased to leave the cats and dogs at last. They put on their shiny brass helmets. They armed themselves with hatchets, pumps, ropes, hooks, and ladders, and in no time were on the football ground. They did not ask their usual question: "Where is the fire?" They only called out "Who's winning?"

The footballers did not answer, but pointed desperately at the balls hovering in the sky. "Leave that to us," said the firemen, "we will soon get them. Our ladder is higher than the highest building in Kickford, which is five storeys high, anyhow."

So they put up their new ladder, and the captain of the fire brigade climbed on to the top to fetch the footballs. The balls did not want to be fetched, but always stayed just out of reach. Then the firemen pulled the ladder and their captain round the field, following the balls. However, the balls dodged very cleverly and teased the fat captain, danced round him, pushed off his helmet, and jumped up and down. When they got tired of him, they went up higher and higher and disappeared in the clouds.

"There is nothing to be done," said the captain of the fire brigade, in disgust and mortification. He wiped his forehead. "We are not meant for the clouds. You will have to call the airmen. They know the sky much better than we do."

So they rang up the aerodrome, and soon three military aeroplanes arrived. The pilots had brought tennis rackets with them, and, leaning out of the planes, tried to hit the footballs down. But the balls did not go down. They only laughed at them, bounced and jumped. Then they hid behind the clouds, which made the airmen furious.

"This is the result of helping civilians," said the commander of the squadron, angrily. "Let them get their footballs themselves." And the pilots flew away.

The footballers were also furious, because they could not continue their game. They started quarrelling amongst themselves. "It is your fault," said Goalbridge to Kickford. "You have done this on purpose, because you knew perfectly well that we should beat you again 10 to 0." "That is a lie," said Kickford. "The Silver Cup was almost ours, because O'Kay has not had a steak for over a week. We would have won for sure, and that is why you made the ball stay in the sky."

"Nonsense," said the Goalbridge captain. "Your O'Kay does not know any more about a football match than my new canary. It surprises me that he puts football boots on at all. You'd better buy a pair of slippers, sir." "Oh," replied O'Kay, gnashing his teeth. "You mean that I don't know anything about football? Just wait and see."

These are the slippers O'Kay should have

He dashed into the crowd, seized a melon which Mr. Pills, the chemist, was holding in his hand, ready to cut up, and he kicked it like a ball straight into the Goalbridge goal.

But the Goalbridge captain followed this up with Mrs. Pills's beautiful knitting bag, and shot it straight into the Kickford goal. And all the footballers, following their example, stormed the stands, seized anything which was at all round in shape, and started kicking them all over the football ground. The heroic Kickford team preferred bowler hats and water melons, while the stalwart Goalbridges got hold of rubber cushions and balloons.

The crowd was now furious; the boys jeered; the Referee blew his whistle in vain; those who had been robbed protested to the Mayors; Mrs. Pills fainted; Mr. Pills called for the police. Only the strong and determined men in the trees, very much amused, shouted: "Keep it going, keep it going." Because, as they were sitting high up in the branches, they felt quite safe from the mad footballers.

However, the hats, the melons, the knitting bags, the balloons, and the rubber cushions did not like being pushed so roughly all over the place. They also flew up into the sky to keep the footballs company, and stayed there with them. And very soon the sky looked like the window of a big store.

The players kept on running hither and thither to get hold of something round to kick. When, however, O'Kay seized the last bowler hat off the head of the Goalbridge Mayor and sent it into the clouds, also . . . there was nothing round left on the whole field except the helmets of the firemen.

So the Goalbridge and Kickford players together rushed towards the firemen, with fierce war cries, to get hold of their shiny helmets. But the firemen sheltered behind their pumps. They took their hoses and greeted the storming footballers with streams of cold water.

The footballers did not like this in the least. They shook the water off and wrung out their shirts very angrily. O'Kay turned on the commander of the fire brigade, and said: "I say, it is a foul, and is against the rules of the game." And the Goalbridge captain, who two minutes ago had been fighting with O'Kay, agreed, and said: "This is very unfair." The rest of the footballers joined them, saying: "Under these conditions we can't get on with the game," and they walked off the field in a rage. The Referee, who also got very wet, said: "I must go home quickly and drink camomile tea, otherwise I will catch a cold." So he took his scooter, and left, grumbling to himself. Then the Mayors together said furiously: "We have been degraded, because our hats have been stolen, and a Mayor without a bowler hat is a Mayor no longer." And they called for their cars, and left, too.

But the crowd stayed in their seats, and shouted: "We are not going home, as we have paid a lot for our tickets and want to see a football match." And louder still shouted the

strong and determined men in the trees, who had not paid a brass farthing, but who had very healthy and powerful lungs, and made good use of them.

"We want football," they cried out. "Return the money!" And it seemed as though they would never stop shouting.

But the little boys, who were now left by themselves in the Mayors' box, listened to the crowd asking for the footballers. They looked at the lovely, empty playground with its straight white lines and goalposts. They thought such a chance would never come again. And so young William O'Kay stepped forward and held up his hand for the crowd to be silent. When there was quiet, he said: "We are footballers, also, and we also can kick the ball quite well. Let us play for the Silver Cup."

The onlookers laughed, and said: "Ha, ha, ha! You are only little boys! Anyway, where is your football?" Young O'Kay proudly answered: "First of all, you are as unjust as are most grown ups, because you have never seen us playing and you do not know how much more difficult it is to play on the bumpy common than on your smooth ground. Besides, we can get our ball whenever we like, because we know how to handle it."

He looked up into the sky, put two fingers into his mouth and whistled three times. His own old, mended football turned round and said to the other football, the melons, hats, knitting bags, balloons, and rubber cushions: "I beg your pardon, but I have to go down now. My master is calling me. His friends are small and nice, and don't kick hard. Stay here awhile and you will see for yourself."

And so he went down, and young O'Kay patted him. The boys started the match. They kicked the football in a friendly way and it soared gently from one goal to the other. The onlookers enjoyed themselves and applauded, and the ball had a good time.

And when the match had to stop because of the darkness, the result was 48. Namely, 24 goals for Goalbridge and 24 goals for Kickford.

The crowd left the stands and trees. Shouting with joy, they ran on to the ground. They lifted the twenty-two little boys on to their shoulders. People said: "We have seen many matches, but never so many goals scored before." And so as a reward for their fine play, they gave the Silver Cup to the boys.

When the hats, melons, knitting bags, rubber cushions, and balloons and the other football saw that there was no longer any danger, down they came, slowly, again. And the boys caught them and gave them back to their owners, all except the melons, which they ate, as they were very thirsty. The brass band played a march. The fire brigade lit their torches and stood in a line, while the heroes of the day were carried home in triumph.

THE *END*